Incredibly
Disgusting
Drugs™

Crystal Meth

Jeremy Harrow

rosen publishing's
**rosen
central**

New York

Published in 2008 by The Rosen Publishing Group, Inc.
29 East 21st Street, New York, NY 10010

Library of Congress Cataloging-in-Publication Data

Harrow, Jeremy.
Crystal meth / Jeremy Harrow. — 1st ed.
   p. cm. — (Incredibly disgusting drugs)
Includes bibliographical references and index.
ISBN-13: 978-1-4042-1953-3 (library binding)
ISBN-10: 1-4042-1953-6 (library binding)
1. Methamphetamine abuse—Juvenile literature. I. Title.
RC568.A45H37 2007
616.86'4–dc22

2007004714

Manufactured in China

Contents

Introduction

Crystal meth is one of the most dangerous drugs on the planet. It's dangerous to take, it's dangerous to make, and it can be dangerous to be around people who are on it. It can turn you into a monster. If you take it long enough, it will make you look like one.

All drugs are bad for you, but crystal meth is the worst of the worst. Do you know how when people see a huge tornado, they turn around and run for their lives? Well, if you see crystal meth coming your way, you should likewise run for your life. It's that dangerous.

Crystal meth is a form of methamphetamine. It has many different nicknames, including "ice," "glass," "crank," and "Tina." Methamphetamine is a super-charged version of another drug called amphetamine. Amphetamines are powerful stimulants that can keep you awake for days if you overuse them. When you add a methyl molecule to its chemical structure, you get methamphetamine. It can be made into a powder, or it can be turned into a solid rock shape. The rocks are far more destructive than the powder. These rocks often have the appearance of white or yellow crystals. This is crystal meth.

Crystal meth won't just change your life; it will change the lives of everyone around you. This is because as you change, your relationship with each of the people in your life will also change.

A hardcore meth addict is not pretty to look at. The drug will destroy you from the inside out. It will be next to impossible for you to keep living a normal life. Meth addicts lose their friends, their jobs, their money, and their sanity. They look like zombies for good reason—they live like them.

The best way to avoid all the disgusting and destructive effects of crystal meth is not to try it at all. One hit of this drug is enough to make you addicted. It is considered by many to be the most addictive drug in the world. Once you are on it, it could take years to get off it. There are only four places you can go when you start taking meth. The lucky ones go to a drug rehabilitation center to break their addiction. The rest will either end up in a hospital, a prison cell, or a cemetery. As you'll see, there are no happy endings for users of crystal meth.

1
Monster
in the Mirror

It's sometimes hard for drug addicts to see the changes in themselves over a long period of time. They either don't want to see them, or they just don't care. The only thing they're likely thinking about is getting high again. It's pretty hard to see your situation clearly when you're high. It's even harder when the drug you're using is crystal meth. For this reason, users will ignore the monster in the mirror. Anyone else can see the changes, which can make you sick to your stomach to look at.

Before and After

People who are addicted to crystal meth look like they've been chewed up and spit out. Their physical appearance gets so bad that they look almost like entirely different people. Their appearance is so gross and disgusting that their pictures are often the best weapons in the war against this disgusting drug.

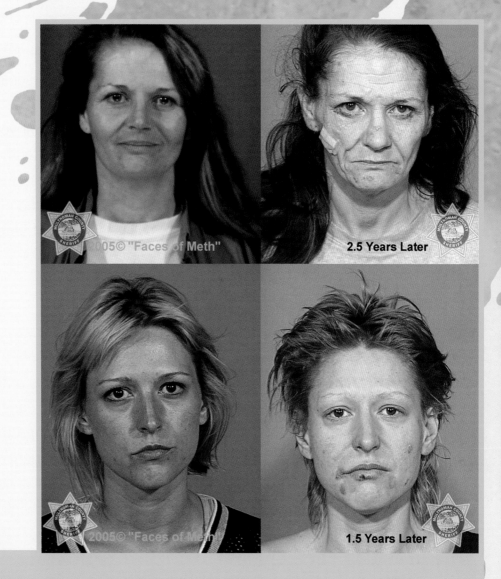

2005© "Faces of Meth"

2.5 Years Later

2005© "Faces of Meth"

1.5 Years Later

Crystal meth is like a vacuum that sucks the life out of a person's face. These mug shots of two meth addicts in Oregon show how much damage the drug does.

Police deputy Bret King in Oregon created a slideshow of mug shots to show students the devastating effects of meth abuse. He named the educational program "Faces of Meth." The mug shots were taken separately over a long span of time. The contrast between the early and later stages of addiction is like night and day. These are faces that will haunt you.

In Illinois, a meth addict named Penny Wood agreed to let authorities use her disturbing before-and-after images on billboards across the state. In the first photo, she appears normal. In the second photo, the effects of meth use are clear. Other states are now using this type of before-and-after approach in antidrug posters.

Extreme Meth Makeover

Crystal meth attacks the body in several distinct and noticeable ways. These symptoms are so recognizable that it becomes pretty easy to spot a meth addict. It's important to remember, though, that not everybody is at the same stage of addiction. So, you might look at someone in the early stage and he or she might look fine. This will almost certainly change for the worse with time. If you use meth long enough, you will experience the terrible symptoms described in the following sections. There is no way to avoid them.

The Changing Face of Meth

A common problem among meth addicts is the many pimples or sores that sprout over their faces. These ugly red invaders show up on other areas of the body, too. They are generally known as speed bumps or

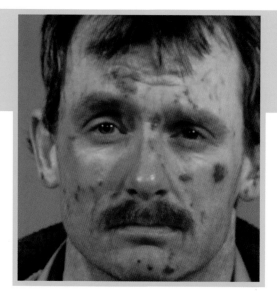

Methamphetamine irritates the surface of the skin. Its effect on the skin tissue made red sores break out on this man's face.

crank sores. The methamphetamine becomes absorbed in the skin, triggering a reaction that produces these bulging blemishes. This skin problem can develop even among occasional users.

Another striking feature of a meth addict's face is the way it seems so lifeless. The skin is thinner and becomes very pale. Eyes turn yellow and look hollow. Meth addicts almost always look much older than their real age. This is because the drug is keeping them awake for days on end. Without sleep, the face deteriorates quickly. The eye sockets sink in. Lines and wrinkles show the wear and tear of years of addiction. Even the addict's hair becomes greasy and mangy. It's like the meth addict has put on a Halloween mask and cannot take it off.

Other Skin Problems

Crystal meth can keep a dermatologist very busy. The skin of a meth user looks like a battlefield. Besides speed bumps, there are lesions.

Some are from the use of needles. One of the ways to get the drug in your body is to shoot it into the skin with a hypodermic needle. This usually leaves a mark, and these marks are called tracks. These areas tend to get infected easily. An addict will shoot up in several different places because each spot will get harder to use from the constant injections.

Meth addicts suffer lots of cuts and bruises. These are usually self-inflicted. The methamphetamine makes the brain react in way that causes people to scratch or pick at themselves for hours. Something as simple as tweezing hair can get very messy. Addicts will keep doing it until they rip their skin open. Therefore, it is not uncommon to see a user with all kinds of scars.

Meth Mouth

Don't ever ask serious meth addicts to smile for the camera. When they open up their mouths, you might want to close your eyes. One of the most disgusting side effects of meth abuse is called meth mouth. Most people who regularly use crystal meth will lose some teeth. Any remaining teeth slowly rot and turn black or a grayish brown. Serious addicts will lose all of their teeth. Gum disease is common among addicts. Their gums loosen and bleed often.

There are various reasons for this gruesome condition. One is that frequent use of crystal meth causes dry mouth. This means there is not enough saliva to protect the mouth from bacteria and harmful acids. Without saliva to act as a shield, your teeth will become brittle and fragile.

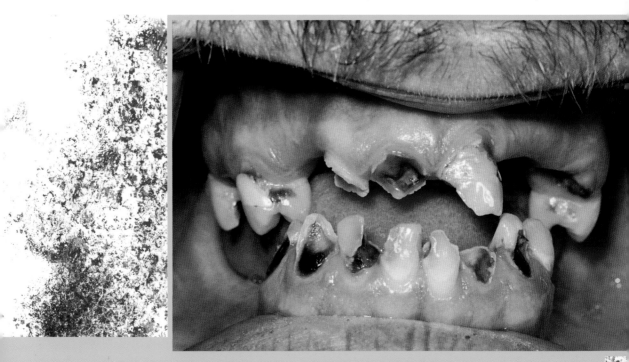

This is a classic example of meth mouth. The toxic chemicals in crystal meth, as well as addicts' neglect of their teeth, cause this to occur.

Another cause of meth mouth is the constant grinding of teeth. Many addicts grind their teeth all the time. They can't stop doing it because they're nervous and restless from being on meth. All this grinding wears down the teeth until they look like twisted stumps.

The biggest reason for meth mouth is that addicts usually stop taking care of their teeth altogether. Getting high becomes more important than brushing or flossing. Addicts also constantly expose their teeth to the toxic chemicals in crystal meth, chemicals like red phosphorus and battery acid. Even if you're young and never had a cavity, meth mouth can still happen to you.

Wasting Away

Crystal meth is not a diet pill, but it will make you keep losing weight until you are skin and bones. Remember, this is an extremely powerful stimulant. It speeds up your metabolism until your body burns off the pounds that you do need. This is not a good thing. Meth won't just kill your appetite. It will kill you, too, from malnutrition.

The reason for the malnutrition is that addicts pump their bodies full of dangerous chemicals instead of food that contains the vital nutrients they need. Crystal meth only makes you crave more meth, not food. You're not just going to become very skinny. Your bones are going to grow weak. Your teeth are going to fall out. Your immune system, which protects you from infections and viruses, is going to collapse. People who were once young and strong end up looking like they belong in a nursing home.

Tweaking

One sure sign of meth addiction is a jittery body. Meth addicts can't sit or stand still. They twitch and shake compulsively as if they were shivering in the freezing cold. This restless behavior is called tweaking. These symptoms are similar to a condition called Parkinson's disease, which causes uncontrollable tremors in a person. The brain and body's reaction to the methamphetamine causes the jerky movements.

The reason for tweaking is that a chemical called dopamine serves a very important role in controlling the body's movements and coordination. People who suffer from Parkinson's have virtually stopped producing dopamine. The nerve cells that produce the dopamine have been permanently damaged. Meth causes similar damage because it compels the brain to make dopamine until the cells are empty. It takes time for these cells to recover and start building up new reserves of dopamine. Without dopamine, the nerve cells are either unable to control a person's muscles or do it very poorly. Over time, the nerve cell damage from the meth will become worse, and in some cases, maybe permanent. A lot of this damage occurs in the same area of the brain called the striatum, which is associated with motor control.

Dopamine

Dopamine is the source of all pleasure in meth addicts. It's a neurotransmitter. A neurotransmitter is a chemical in your brain that carries information from one part to another. Brain cells use neurotransmitters to communicate with each other. All the cells are separated by synaptic fluid. It's kind of like a river, and the neurotransmitters are messengers on boats.

A cell will typically release more neurotransmitters than are necessary. The same cell will then quickly vacuum up the additional neurotransmitters and recycle them for future use.

This meth lab was found in a Texas home. Methamphetamine production is hard to stop because addicts can make it themselves in their homes.

Crystal meth reverses the vacuum so that the cell keeps spitting out dopamine, which then floods the receiving cells. This is what accounts for the unbelievable feeling of euphoria that overcomes methamphetamine users, as you'll read in the next chapter.

Dopamine has many important purposes. It's vital to the central nervous system. It helps control motions. Dopamine also makes you enjoy an activity. It's the biggest motivation to do the activity again.

Smell You Later

Crystal meth users usually take poor care of themselves. They don't just neglect their teeth. They neglect everything: hair, armpits, fingernails, toenails, hands, and ears. If it can get dirty, they probably don't remember to clean it. This is all part of what happens when the only thing you can think about is using meth and getting more of it. It's also because the drug damages one's sense of smell. Addicts can't really tell that they're neglecting their hygiene.

When police enter the home of a meth addict, it's usually overflowing with trash. The only thing more disgusting is the stench of the meth being cooked up in a meth lab, where the drug is created using various dangerous chemicals. It has a funky odor that's been compared to cat urine and dead bodies. Sometimes a house has to be demolished because of the smell. It's that strong.

Take a Good Look

Now that you know what a crystal meth user looks like, go in front of a mirror. You look young and healthy, right? Now imagine all the nasty things that can happen because of meth. Being young and healthy will not protect you from those things. If you use meth, you will look like it.

2
Going Out
of Your **Mind**

Nowhere is the damage worse from crystal meth than in the brain. What happens in the brain is why people use meth and why they become so addicted to it. Meth can make you feel incredible and dynamic, but that's only a temporary sensation. It's a short way up, but it's a long way down. Feelings of pleasure and power are replaced by severe depression, insomnia, hallucinations, and paranoia. It won't happen overnight, but it will happen. These side effects won't go away. Once crystal meth gets in your brain, it will change your personality in ways that you could never imagine.

Why Do People Do It?

Crystal meth may be the most addictive drug on the planet because it causes the brain to release much more dopamine than other drugs. Users feel so much pleasure that they want to keep reliving the experience. They crave it more than anything. When they use crystal

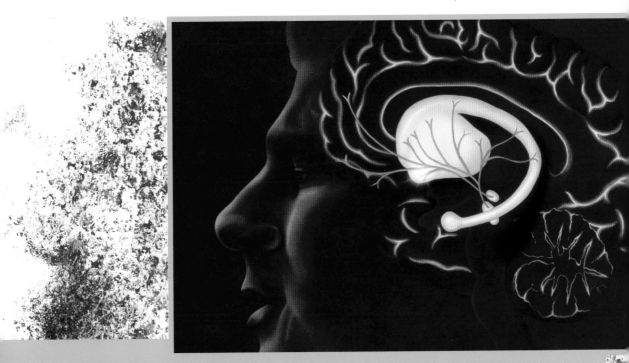

Crystal meth sets off a flood of dopamine in a person's brain that can lead to addiction. Other drugs, like cocaine, ecstasy, and marijuana, operate on the same reward system.

meth, they are rewarded with pleasure. Soon, they feel like they can't live without it. Nothing else will feel as good to them. This is the nature of addiction. To understand this reward system, you'll need to know about two areas of the brain and dopamine.

Nucleus Accumbens

When James Brown sang, "I feel good," it was the nucleus accumbens making him feel that way. It makes everyone feel good. It's located around the lower forebrain, near the midbrain. This is where your sense of pleasure comes from. When the taste of food or the rhythm of music makes you feel good, it's because of all the dopamine in your nucleus accumbens.

Ventral Tegmental Area

We know when we feel good, but what tells the nucleus accumbens to make us feel that way? The answer is the ventral tegmental area (VTA). The VTA is located in the midbrain. This is the part of the brain that makes us know we want something or appreciate something. The craving or desire starts here. The VTA then tells the nucleus accumbens to enjoy the thing that we crave so much. It also has the dopamine to send to the nucleus accumbens. The message is in the dopamine.

The Reward System

Crystal meth takes over the reward system in your brain. This is why it's so addictive. Crystal meth stimulates the VTA. This is where we learn to crave a substance. It's also where there's dopamine that will help motivate the user to keep taking meth. The VTA sends the dopamine to the nucleus accumbens. The dopamine stimulates the nucleus accumbens to feel pleasure. Crystal meth forces the VTA to keep shooting out dopamine until it's empty. The nucleus accumbens gets so much dopamine that the crystal meth user feels a tidal wave of pleasure.

From Feeling Good to Feel Bad

Most people like to keep doing things that feel good to them. You might have a favorite song that you listen to all the time. This is normal. However, there are other things that might seem enjoyable, but they can actually make you feel much worse. Have you ever been to an all-you-can-eat restaurant, eaten as much as you could, and felt sick afterwards? This is because you ate more food than your body needed and was used to. So, maybe you got a stomachache, or maybe you wanted to throw up.

Crystal meth shoots off too much dopamine in your brain. The nucleus accumbens becomes an all-you-can-enjoy dopamine feast. This is not normal. You would never release this much dopamine on your own. Once you get used to that much pleasure, you won't be able to enjoy anything else. It also messes with all your other brain activity. It can lead to severe depression, insomnia, hallucinations, and paranoia.

Severe Depression

Crystal meth will keep you high for a long time before the dopamine runs out. It can last up to twelve hours or longer. Do you know what happens to a plane when it runs out of fuel? It crashes. The same thing happens to your brain when the meth has wiped out all of the dopamine. You crash and sink into a depression. A depression is a mental condition that is associated with feelings of intense sadness and hopelessness.

Crystal meth brings on depression in many addicts. It takes time for the brain to restore a normal level of serotonin and dopamine.

The more you use meth, the worse the depression will get during each crash. This is because it takes the brain longer and longer to resupply new batches of dopamine. Crystal meth also damages another neurotransmitter, serotonin. Serotonin plays an important role in your overall mood. You won't want to get out of bed if you don't have enough dopamine or serotonin. You won't want to do anything. People who suffer from severe depression sometimes become suicidal. This means they don't want to live. You'll need to keep taking meth to feel good about yourself.

Insomnia

One thing about being on crystal meth is that you will not sleep for days or even a week if you take too much of it. Insomnia is the inability to get the proper amount of sleep. It's usually caused by stress, panic attacks, or too much caffeine, like in coffee. In this case, it's because a person is bouncing off the walls from using meth.

The meth causes two neurotransmitters, glutamate and norepinephrine, to work overtime. Glutamate is responsible for your being awake and alert. Norepinephrine makes you focus; it also helps give you energy in stressful situations. Meth stimulates your brain so that these two neuro-transmitters keep going and going. This is why you aren't able to sleep. It might not sound bad, but without sleep for this long a period, you'll be ready to jump out of your skin.

This type of extreme insomnia is very destructive. Sleep is important because it gives the body a chance

Insomnia diminishes a person's memory and concentration. Lack of sleep makes it hard to think straight. Addicts who stay awake for days may also hallucinate.

to rest and repair itself. This is why people sleep a lot when they get sick. So, if you don't sleep, your chances of catching an illness are greatly increased.

The other big problem is that when you finally crash from being up so long, you end up sleeping for several consecutive days to make up the time. You won't be able to lead a normal life. You'll be like a vampire that turns into a mummy.

Hallucinations

Hallucinations are nightmares you experience when you're wide awake. You see bad things that seem real, but they're only in your mind. You can hear scary voices, too, when you hallucinate. These voices are coming from inside your brain. They're not real.

You also can have emotional hallucinations. These happen when you experience a feeling or emotion that isn't real. You might get very angry with your friend, even though your friend didn't do anything to make you mad. The reason for hallucinations is that meth damages the parts of the brain that help you tell the difference between reality and fantasy. It alters your perception.

People who abuse meth have horrible hallucinations of having insects crawling all over their skin. These are sometimes called meth bugs. Addicts will scratch their arms or legs until they bleed.

Paranoia

Paranoid people think something bad is always about to happen to them. They think the police are about to arrest them. They think strangers are

ARMS OF A TENNESSEE METH USER

METH BUGS

SHE KNOWS THEY'RE NOT REAL,
BUT IT DOESN'T STOP HER FROM TRYING
TO PICK THEM OUT OF HER SKIN.

METH
DESTROYS

Meth users often think they have bugs swarming over them. These hallucinations are so convincing that some addicts rip their skin open.

following them. They think their family wants to hurt them. It doesn't matter if it's true or not. They only believe what they want to believe. Crystal meth makes people very paranoid. It's part of the overall brain damage that also causes hallucinations. The thin line between what's real and what's imaginary is no longer there.

Paranoid behavior can often lead to violence. This is common among meth addicts. They might attack their own children. They might hurt themselves. It all depends on how severe their paranoia is at the time. Remember, they haven't slept, they're depressed, and they're hearing voices. Nothing is real to them anymore.

3
The
Dark Side
of Addiction

Crystal meth won't just make you look terrible and act strangely. It will take over your life as well. If you become addicted, the only thing that will concern you is getting more meth. It won't matter that your teeth are falling out or you're seeing things that don't exist. Being an addict is like being a slave. You will do whatever it takes to satisfy those powerful cravings. Nothing will be more important than your next hit of the drug. This is the dark side of addiction. People will give up everything to get high.

Crime

It's impossible to not be a criminal when you become a meth addict. As with most drugs, it's a crime to possess, sell, or make meth. However, there are other crimes related to the drug.

Crystal meth damages the amygdala, the emotional center of the brain. Addicts have little or no control over their temper.

Stealing

There are many names for stealing. Robbery, burglary, shoplifting, and grand larceny are a few. Addiction is expensive, and crystal meth isn't free. What if you're broke? Nobody is just going to keep lending you money. Besides, you need it now. Your body is craving meth, and it won't stop. This is why many addicts start stealing from family and friends. They then move on to shoplifting and breaking into people's homes.

Abuse and Violence

Crystal meth makes people's behavior very unpredictable. It interferes with all the parts of the brain that control emotions and good judgment. The line between right and wrong is blurred. This causes addicts to act in ways that are unacceptable. They are quicker to attack if they lose their temper. They can be physically and verbally abusive. This can happen in their home and even out in public.

Homicide

It doesn't take much for meth addicts to turn to homicide, especially if they're paranoid and haven't slept for a week. All it takes is a deadly weapon, like a gun or a knife. The results are often tragic.

The police are sometimes the targets. In Oklahoma, a man named Ricky Ray Malone shot a state trooper. Malone killed the trooper with the officer's own gun. He had been cooking meth out in the open when the trooper came by. This and the meth-related murders of other policemen prompted Oklahoma to pass the toughest law against meth in the nation.

Meth in the Home

Many addicts prefer to cook up their own meth. They will actually cook it in their own home. This is unsafe for everyone living in the home because crystal meth is made from toxic chemicals. These materials are also extremely flammable. They can cause a fiery explosion that kills anyone who is close by. To remove the threat, the police have to call in special units to take apart these meth labs. Those in the special units have to cover themselves in protective gear.

A "meth home" suffers in other ways, too:

- Cooking up meth produces a foul odor that makes the whole place smell rotten.
- Children are often neglected and abused.
- Piles of garbage are everywhere.
- Insects and rodents infest the home.
- Everyone breathes in the unsafe fumes of the cooking meth.

Poisoning Your Body

Crystal meth is made from poison. It's like cooking dinner in a chemistry lab. There are no natural ingredients. Almost every ingredient is toxic. No one would ever swallow, smoke, snort, or inject any of them separately. People who cook meth know these ingredients and put them in their bodies despite

Lye is a poisonous chemical found in drain cleaners and laundry detergents. Anhydrous ammonia is a powerful fertilizer that is used in crop production.

the risk. Chemicals become their diet. Meth kills their appetite for food. It's not unusual for police to find empty refrigerators when they raid a meth lab.

Imagine a daily diet of these ingredients:

- Mercury
- Anhydrous ammonia
- Lye
- Hydrochloric acid
- Toluene
- Methanol
- Ether
- Battery acid
- Red phosphorus

When these ingredients get together, it's not a picnic. It's a recipe for disaster.

Turning Into a Stranger

Meth addicts undergo major transformations. Their lives turn upside down. They become strangers to their families and friends. It's a painful experience for everyone involved. No one enjoys watching their father, mother, son, daughter, brother, sister, best friend, boyfriend, or girlfriend throw their life away. They will have to sit by and watch them lose their teeth, act crazily, steal money, and turn violent.

Meth and the Younger Brother

Mary F. Holley knows what crystal meth did to her younger brother, Jim. It made him paranoid. He thought drug dealers were after him. Meth made him hallucinate all the time.

Mary tried to help Jim. She let him stay with her. Then she got him an apartment. She also found him a job. It didn't matter. He lost his job. He couldn't pay his bills. He had to be bailed out of jail. Everything kept getting worse. Jim committed suicide in 2000. He was only twenty-four years old. After her brother's death, Mary founded Mothers Against Methamphetamine to help educate people about the dangers of meth.

The Young Mom on Meth

Brittany Bowman used to take her young son to meth labs. Today, as a recovering addict, she can't believe her crazy behavior on meth. She felt like a monster. She knew how dangerous it was to be around a meth lab, but she was too addicted to care.

Brittany started using meth when she was seventeen years old. She had quit once before during her pregnancy. She got her life together. Then one day, she got hooked again. It only took her a few months to lose her job, her apartment, her car, and custody of her son. She would sometimes be up for six days, and then she would sleep for two. Eventually she got off meth for good.

Wasting Away on Meth

Not many eighteen-year-olds can move out on their own with a $15,000 inheritance in their pocket. For Michael Reichman, it was a dream come true. He moved into an apartment with a friend and was ready to take on the world. What he wasn't ready for was a full-blown addiction to crystal meth. His dream life soon became a nightmare. He spent every cent he had on meth until he was homeless. He became incredibly paranoid. He lost so much weight that his bones were sticking out. The addiction chased away his friends and terrified his family. It took a long time, but he finally got off the drug.

One Addict, Many Addictions

Crystal meth is usually not somebody's first drug. There's a good chance that they've already tried others, like marijuana, or sniffed glue. Sometimes it starts with cigarettes. It's also usually not the person's only addiction.

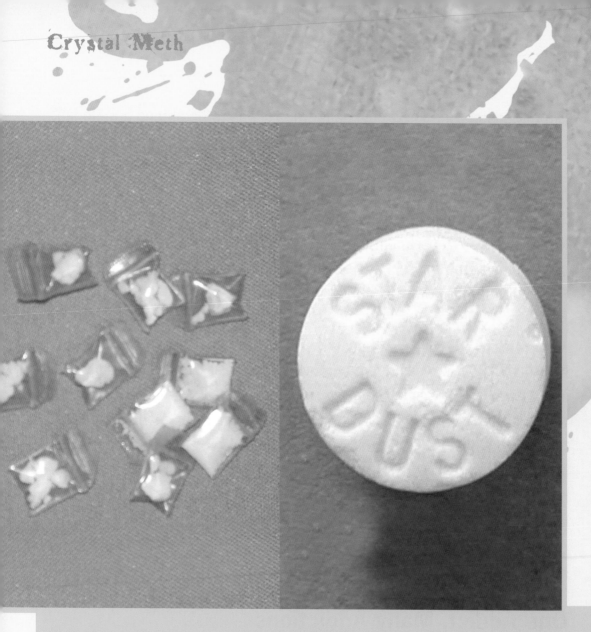

Cocaine (*left*) and ecstasy are just some of the other drugs that meth addicts often try. Cocaine is a highly addictive stimulant, and the high from ecstasy is almost identical to that of meth.

You can get addicted to more than one drug at a time. It just becomes part of the whole lifestyle.

Addicts tend to hang out with other addicts. There's a lot of access to other illegal substances such as cocaine, ecstasy, GHB, and heroin. If you run out of one thing, you're more likely to do another to stay high. Multiple addictions do additional damage to the body and the mind.

Alcohol can be very addictive. It reacts with the brain to release dopamine. Alcohol also strips away self-control and, like meth, causes depression.

Alcohol and Meth

Alcohol helps relieve some of the stressful side effects of doing meth. Alcohol relaxes the body instead of constantly stimulating it like meth does. It makes you sleepier. It's not unusual for meth addicts to also be alcoholics. They might have already been alcoholics. Drinking can set up the mind to be more open to addictive substances. People might take their first hit of meth when they're drunk. Alcoholism will cause even more damage to the brain and the liver.

Speedballs

Speedballs are cocaine mixed with heroin, morphine, or an amphetamine such as meth. They're popular with a lot of meth addicts. The combination acts like a powerful painkiller in your body. It's also very lethal.

Many people die from overdosing on speedballs. It's difficult to break the habit of just one drug, but together, the user may never fully recover.

4
Permanent Damage

s it worth taking one hit of crystal meth just to see what it feels like? Absolutely not! The person offering it to you might tell you it's the most amazing feeling in the world. We know that dopamine brings pleasure, and we know that meth forces the brain to use all of it. Some people might be tempted to try meth once or twice because they think they can stop anytime. Well, lots of hospitals, drug rehabilitation centers, prisons, homeless shelters, and cemeteries are filling up with people who thought they could stop. Those people are never going to be the same again. They can get clean, but the damage has already been done. They can only try to live the best life possible as a recovering meth addict. For those in the cemetery, it's too late.

Health Problems

Years or even months of drug abuse are hard on the body. Addicts spend more time putting toxic substances into their system than food or vitamins. If nothing good is going in, then nothing good is going to happen.

Crystal meth is harmful to your internal organs. The complications to your health can be severe and potentially deadly. You can develop chronic problems in vital organs, like your heart and brain. You might also contract a serious transmittable disease such as AIDS or hepatitis.

The Heart

Your heart is like the engine of your body. Using crystal meth is like pushing on the accelerator of a car and never letting up. Any stimulant makes your body work extremely fast. Methamphetamines make you go the fastest—so fast that it can burn out your heart.

Meth makes your blood pressure go way up, too. High blood pressure makes it harder for your blood to be pushed through your circulatory system. The effect of so much dopamine being released causes your blood vessels to get smaller. On top of all this, your heart is beating so fast that it needs more blood. If it doesn't get enough, you can die of a heart attack. It can happen at any time. The longer you do meth, the greater the risk.

Meth can also lead to heart failure. Your heart muscles get weaker from the chemicals. Your blood gets backed up because the heart is so weak. You'll find yourself more out of breath. You won't be able to do much. It can take years off your life. You'll never undo this kind of damage. You can only prevent it by not doing meth.

A meth addict who has a heart attack will end up in the emergency room. A team of doctors will try to shock the heart back into a normal rhythm by using a defibrillator.

Hemorrhages

When you think of bleeding, you probably think of minor cuts on your skin that can be healed with a Band-Aid. Meth can cause a different kind of bleeding. It can make you suffer a hemorrhage, which is internal bleeding that occurs when blood spills out of an artery into the surrounding area. Meth is full of toxic chemicals that can destroy your blood vessels, including the arteries. Have you ever seen anyone cough up blood? It's not pretty. Imagine seeing blood in your urine. These hemorrhages can cause strokes, kidney failure, stomach pains, ulcers, and death.

Your Lungs

A lot of people smoke crystal meth. Others inhale the toxic fumes during the cooking process. All of this is bad for their lungs. Many meth addicts also smoke marijuana and cigarettes. Their immune systems are already weak from the insomnia and poor diet. This means their lungs will not be strong enough to fight off infections. Those infections can turn into life-threatening illnesses, like pneumonia. Other lung problems include bronchitis and emphysema. These make it harder to breathe. Many addicts develop a chronic cough. They just cough all the time and are always spitting up mucus.

Parkinson's Disease

The twitches and tremors that are common in meth users are similar to the ones caused by Parkinson's disease. Parkinson's is related to low levels of dopamine. Crystal meth damages the production of dopamine by forcing the brain to use too much of the chemical. Dopamine doesn't just send the message of pleasure. It's also responsible for helping the body control its movements. Some addicts will continue to twitch and shake even after they get clean. They may be more likely to develop Parkinson's disease at a younger age.

Transmittable Diseases

Transmittable diseases are ones that are passed between people. They are transmitted through the exchange of blood or other bodily fluids. There are two ways that addicts catch these diseases. One is by sharing intravenous needles to inject meth. The other is by engaging in risky sexual activity. Both of these forms of transmission are common among meth users. The more serious of these diseases are AIDS and hepatitis. There is no cure for either. Both can shorten your life. Other transmittable diseases include herpes, gonorrhea, chlamydia, and syphilis.

Mental and Emotional Problems

Crystal meth interferes with the neurotransmitters that control your moods and feelings. It takes a long time to clean up the mess that meth makes in your brain. You don't just return to normal when you quit using the drug. Your brain has to try to repair the damage. This can take years. Some damage can never be fixed. Many recovering addicts cannot function because of the depression that meth causes. They may need to be on antidepressants for the rest of their lives.

Criminal Record

Many addicts end up behind bars. It could be for meth, or it could be for crimes they committed while high on meth. A criminal record will follow

Children who live with meth addicts are often abused and neglected. These kids may be taken away from their parents and placed in foster homes.

addicts for the rest of their lives. It will show up on any background check for a future job. A lot of companies will not hire a convicted criminal. There are also companies that have strict antidrug policies. They may not trust a former drug addict. Many former prisoners will go back to their old ways because they can't find a good job. It becomes a cycle, and they end up right back in jail.

Broken Relationships

Addiction doesn't just destroy brain cells. It tears apart families. It breaks up marriages. It ruins friendships. Addiction brings out the worst in people. It causes them to hurt the ones closest to them. Meth makes good people do bad things. Parents might neglect and abuse their children. Children might lie and steal from their parents. Siblings may become violent with each other. Best friends may become strangers. There is a loss of trust and respect. Can these relationships ever be repaired? There is no easy answer. Some people cannot forgive and forget. Hurt feelings can take a long time to heal.

A Lifetime Struggle

Crystal meth is a powerful drug with a tight grip. Treatment and recovery can take years. Many addicts quit and then start again. The withdrawal process is excruciating. The mind and body have to learn how to function without meth again. This makes people very sick and depressed. They will feel worse than ever. Getting high again will be a major temptation. A lot of people can't do it. The addiction is too strong. They will use meth until they end up in jail or die. For those who can get clean, it will be a lifetime struggle.

Glossary

addict A person who becomes so used to doing something that he can't stop doing it on his own.

amphetamine A drug that causes a person to have lots of energy and to stay awake.

depression An overwhelming feeling of sadness and hopelessness.

dopamine The neurotransmitter that is responsible for the feeling of pleasure in a person.

hallucinations Imaginary visions and sounds.

meth mouth A condition among meth addicts that causes rotting teeth and bleeding gums.

methamphetamine A powerful amphetamine that can be made into a powder or crystals. It causes the brain to release massive amounts of dopamine.

neurotransmitter A chemical in the brain that carries information from one part to another.

nucleus accumbens The area of the brain that rewards a person with feelings of pleasure.

paranoia When a person is obsessed with the idea that someone or something is out to get him.

ventral tegmental The area of the brain that causes a person to crave something.

For More Information

Drug Abuse Resistance Education (D.A.R.E.)
9800 La Cienega Boulevard, Suite 401
Inglewood, CA 90301
(800) 223-DARE (223-3273)
Web site: http://www.dare.com

Drug Free America Foundation
2600 9th Street N., Suite 200
St. Petersburg, FL 33704
(727) 828-0211
Web site: http://www.dfaf.org/studentsection

National Institute on Drug Abuse
6001 Executive Boulevard, Room 5213
Bethesda, MD 20892-9561
(301) 443-1124
Web site: http://www.teens.drugabuse.gov

Partnership for a Drug-Free America
405 Lexington Avenue, Suite 1601
New York, NY 10174
(212) 922-1560
Web site: http://www.drugfree.org

Students Against Destructive Decisions (SADD)
255 Main Street
Marlborough, MA 01752
(877) SADD-INC (723-3462)
Web site: http://www.sadd.org

White House Office of National Drug Control Policy
Drug Policy Information Clearinghouse
P.O. Box 6000
Rockville, MD 20849-6000
(800) 666-3332
Web site: http://www.whitehousedrugpolicy.gov

Web Sites

Due to the changing nature of Internet links, Rosen Publishing has developed an online list of Web sites related to the subject of this book. This site is updated regularly. Please use this link to access the list:

http://www.rosenlinks.com/idd/crme

For Further Reading

Brady, Betty. *Meth Survivor: Jennifer's Story*. Bloomington, IN: Authorhouse, 2006.

Burgess, Melvin. *Smack*. New York, NY: Avon Tempest, 1999.

Cobb, Allan B. *Speed and Your Brain: The Incredibly Disgusting Story*. New York, NY: Rosen Publishing, 2003.

Hopkins, Ellen. *Crank*. New York, NY: Simon Pulse, 2004.

Mintzer, Rich. *Meth & Speed = Busted!* Berkeley Heights, NJ: Enslow Publishers, 2005.

Spalding, Frank. *Methamphetamine: The Dangers of Crystal Meth*. New York, NY: Rosen Publishing, 2007.

Bibliography

Bowman, Brittany. "The Tightest Grip." The Partnership for a Drug-Free America. Retrieved December 16, 2006 (http://www.drugfree.org/Portal/Stories/The_Tightest_Grip).

Braswell, Sterling R. *American Meth: A History of the Methamphetamine Epidemic in America*. Lincoln, NE: iUniverse, 2005.

Davey, Monica. "Grisly Effect of One Drug: 'Meth Mouth.'" *New York Times*, June 11, 2005. Retrieved December 6, 2006 (http://www.nytimes.com/2005/06/11/national/11meth.htm?ex=1276142400&en= d2ce61d667005d47&ei= 5088&partner=rssnyt&emc=rss).

Holley, Mary F. *Crystal Meth: They Call It Ice*. Mustang, OK: Tate Publishing, 2005.

Johnson, Dirk. *Meth: The Home-Cooked Menace*. Center City, MN: Hazelden, 2005.

Lee, Steven J. *Overcoming Crystal Meth Addiction: An Essential Guide to Getting Clean*. New York, NY: Marlowe & Company, 2006.

Reichman, Michael. "I Looked Like a Dead Person." The Partnership for a Drug-Free America. Retrieved December 16, 2006 (http://www.drugfree.org/Portal/Stories/I_Looked_Like_a_Dead_Person).

Index

About the Author

Jeremy Harrow is a writer from Fort Myers, FL. He has a bachelor's degree in media and communications. As a former community reporter, Harrow has experience writing about national news from a local perspective. He is especially grateful to Dr. Mary F. Holley, the founder of Mothers Against Methamphetamine, for the valuable insight in her book, *Crystal Meth: They Call It Ice*.

Photo Credits

Cover, p. 1 www.istockphoto.com/Nicholas Monu; pp. 7, 9 Multnomah County Sheriff's Office; p. 11 courtesy Christopher Heringlake, D.D.S.; p. 15 FBI Houston HIDTA Methamphetamine Initiative Group (MIG); pp. 17, 40 © Custom Medical Stock Photo; p. 20 www.istockphoto.com/Marcel Pelletier; p. 21 www.istockphoto.com/Jitalia17; p. 23 www.MethFreeTN.org; p. 26 www.istockphoto.com/Nuno Silva; p.29 (left) www.istockphoto.com/Robert Kyllo; p. 29 (right) www.istockphoto.com/DHuss; p. 32 Drug Enforcement Administration; p. 33 www.istockphoto.com/ericsphotography; p. 37 © Will & Deni McIntyre/Photo Researchers, Inc.

Editor: Nicholas Croce; **Designer:** Les Kanturek; **Photo Researcher:** Amy Feinberg